D0599528

Every year at Christmastime, the United States Postal Service receives hundreds of thousands of letters addressed to the same person: Santa Claus, North Pole. To help Santa with all these letters, Postmaster General Frank Hitchcock in 1912 authorized postal workers to work with charities, companies, and individual citizens throughout the United States in what has become the Letters to Santa program. Some local post offices assist Santa by responding to the letters. Others work with groups to collect gifts. Still other post offices invite the public to help Santa answer the letters from children and their families. One hundred years later, volunteer postal workers remain committed to making children's Christmas wishes come true.

Letters to Santa is an annual holiday tradition embraced by the U.S. Postal Service and the public alike. To learn more about this program, or to sign up to adopt letters yourself this Christmas, visit www.usps.com.

© 2012 United States Postal Service

All Rights reserved.

No part of this book may be reproduced, stored in a retrieval system, or transmitted in any form or by any means, electronic, mechanical, photocopying, recording, or otherwise, without the prior permission of the United States Postal Service.

Letters to Santa is produced by becker&mayer!, Bellevue, Washington
www.beckermayer.com

Published in the United States by Pearson Learning Solutions, a Pearson Education Company
501 Boylston St., Suite 900, Boston, MA 02116

Editor: Delia Greve
Designer: Megan Sugiyama
Product Developer: Todd Rider
Production Coordinator: Tom Miller
Managing Editor: Amelia Riedler

With special thanks to Michael Vaccaro and Karen Whitehouse at Pearson Learning Solutions.

Printed, manufactured, and assembled in Shenzhen, China 6/12
Conforms to CPSIA standards.

10 9 8 7 6 5 4 3 2 1

ISBN: 9781256686255
11162

Image credits:
Introduction: Old manuscript page © Vangelis76/Shutterstock; retro banner © candycatdesigns/Shutterstock. Envelope: Santa coat and belt © Kirsty Pargeter/Shutterstock.

LETTERS TO SANTA

From:

to: Santa Claus

North Pole

Written by Deborah Halverson

Illustrated by Pauline Siewert

Carolers sing, silver bells ring, and snow dances lightly across frosted windowpanes. That time of year is here again—it's Christmastime.

Hopeful children gather paper, pencils, and crayons.
It's time to share their Christmas wishes—it's time
to write to Santa.

Up and down the streets, the Christmas spirit turns postal carriers into Santa's eager helpers. Rain? Sleet? Snow? No matter! Postal workers won't let winter weather stop them from gathering the precious Christmas letters.

Wishes come in all kinds of letters. Letters with lists and questions, news, and reindeer hellos. Letters saying "Please" and "Thank you." And letters asking for gifts for others who need them more.

Dear Santa,

How are you? We are in first grade. Our bus goes past a car that a girl lives in. Vance says maybe you can't find someone who doesn't have an address. We made a map. The blue square is the car. The girl can have one of the pirate ships we asked for. We can share the other one.

From your friends,
Darin and Vance

There are letters in every size and color. Really big letters. Little-bitty letters. Letters with stickers and glittery ink. And there are some letters with no words at all—just bright and colorful pictures.

No matter how the letters are written, Santa can tell what's in every child's heart. He knows every wish and that every letter is as special as the child who sends it.

Dear Santa,

My Christmas wish is for Sophia B. to have a jacket. She has just a sweater to wear. We want to play hopscotch at recess, but she gets too cold. She would look pretty in a purple jacket like mine. The pockets are really big and good for holding stuff. Thank you.

Love,
Katie

When the writing is done, it's time to stuff and seal, address and mail. The letter is ready to go . . . all the way to Santa Claus at the North Pole.

ho ho ho ho ho ho ho

Dear Santa,

I was good this year. Well,
    sometimes I was bad, but I
didn't mean it. Like that time
with the egg and Pop's hammer.

    That was an accident. Can I
    have a skateboard like

    Kenji next door? He said you
are getting him one. I promise to
always wear a helmet when I ride
it. Thank you. You're #1!

                    Kirk

From a mailbag to a truck to a large postal building, the letter's journey continues.

Down a conveyor belt, packages, letters, and Christmas wishes ride. Letters go one way and packages go another. *WHOOSH!*

A few more conveyor belts, a little more sorting . . .

. . . and Santa's letters are ready for the longest part of their trip.

Written by children of every age, from every street in every city and town, the letters are boxed tight and loaded up.

Everyone's Christmas wishes come together
for a special flight across the starry sky.

Santa's elves know just what to do when those letters land. Lift! Stack! Pull! Dump! With all their might, they haul the Christmas wishes to Santa's workshop.

All year long, the elves have sharpened their tools,
mixed their paints, and measured their ribbons.
They're ready to make ships that sail, skateboards that zoom,
coats with cozy pockets, and dolls with bright pink bows.

As the elves set to work, Santa reads every letter,
checking his list so he knows who's been naughty
and who's been nice.

Once every letter has been read—and every gift has been made—the elves load up the sleigh with care. They send Santa on his way with a cheer!

Across the starry sky, the reindeer pull Santa's
dashing gold sleigh.

One by one, house by house, Santa lands on snow-dusted rooftops.

S anta's bag is filled with gifts.
He has a gift for every boy
and girl— just the right gift for
every Christmas wish.